Arthur Plays the Blues

A Marc Brown ARTHUR Chapter Book

Arthur Plays the Blues

Text by Stephen Krensky
Based on a teleplay by Catherine Lieuwen

LITTLE, BROWN AND COMPANY
New York An AOL Time Warner Company

First Edition

Text has been reviewed and assigned a reading level by Laurel S. Ernst, M.A., Teachers College, Columbia University, New York, New York; reading specialist, Chappaqua, New York.

ISBN 0-316-12586-5 (hc) / ISBN 0-316-12314-5 (pb)

10 9 8 7 6 5 4 3 2 1

WOR (hc)
COM-MO (pb)

Printed in the United States of America

For all the talented students at the
South Shore Conservatory in Hingham

Chapter 1

"Wonderful, Arthur!" said Mrs. Cardigan.

"Really?"

"Absolutely. And I should know." Mrs. Cardigan was Arthur's piano teacher, the only one he had ever had. "Your fingers are flowing with the keys. Sometimes lightly, sometimes with vigor and strength. But always with feeling."

Arthur played a few more notes.

"Excellent," Mrs. Cardigan went on. "You've really got 'Edelweiss' down pat! If I close my eyes, I can see myself in the Austrian Alps." She took a deep breath. "Goodness, that air is fresh."

Arthur smiled. "Should I try the left hand now?"

"In a minute, dear." Mrs. Cardigan opened her eyes and pushed back a strand of her gray hair. "We have to talk about something first."

"I know, I know," said Arthur. "It's about the other piece. I promise I'll practice it for next time."

Mrs. Cardigan sighed. "Ah, next time . . . That's what we have to talk about. I'm afraid there won't be a next time. You see, I'm retiring."

Arthur gasped. "You're *what*?"

She stood up and went into the kitchen. "I should have told you before," she called out, "but I kept putting it off in case I changed my mind."

Arthur blinked a few times. "But you haven't? Changed your mind, I mean?"

"No." Mrs. Cardigan shook her head. "It's the right thing for me to do."

Arthur frowned. "But I thought only old people retired."

"That's sweet, Arthur," said Mrs. Cardigan, returning with a plate of cookies. "But the fact is, I *am* old, or at least a long way from being young. And there are other things I want to do besides teach piano." She handed him a cookie. "Here . . . They're chocolate chip, your favorite."

Arthur always looked forward to cookies at the end of his lesson, at least until today. He took one to be polite, but he didn't even taste it when he took a bite.

"What will happen to me?" asked Arthur. "I'll never get to Carnegie Hall without your help."

Mrs. Cardigan patted him on the shoulder. "Don't be so sure about that. Your new teacher is actually a concert pianist."

"My new teacher?" Arthur repeated.

Mrs. Cardigan clasped her hands with excitement. "That's right. I've been saving

the good news for last! I've made some calls, and you're going to be taught by none other than . . ." She pointed to a poster on the wall of a long-haired man hunched over a grand piano. "Dr. Frederique Fugue."

Arthur examined the poster closely. Dr. Fugue's expression was very serious. Even his fingers looked serious, perched over the piano keys like an eagle's talons.

"That's him?" Arthur gulped.

"Indeed it is," said Mrs. Cardigan. "Dr. Fugue is very experienced. He's in high demand for concerts, but he always saves time for a few special students. 'One generation must light the way for the next,' he likes to say."

Arthur sighed. "Well, he may be great, but I'll bet his cookies aren't as good as yours."

Chapter 2

Arthur hoped that a good night's sleep would make him feel better about Mrs. Cardigan's news. Unfortunately, it didn't. The next morning his head was still in a swirl. So he went off to the playground thinking a little fresh air might do him some good.

He was hanging upside down from the monkey bars when Binky appeared before him.

"Your face is getting red," said Binky.

"That's the blood rushing to my head," said Arthur. "I'm hoping that will help."

"Help what?"

Arthur swung back around so that he could look at Binky right-side up. "My piano teacher, Mrs. Cardigan, is retiring. The news is making me dizzy."

"She's the one who bakes the great cookies, right?" Binky frowned. "No wonder you're upset."

"It's not just that," said Arthur. "Everything with Mrs. Cardigan was so comfortable. I know she liked me, and I liked her, too. She didn't give me too much to practice or too little, either. Everything was just right. Now I have to start over." He sighed. "And I'm worried about my new teacher."

"You already know who it is?"

"Oh, yes." Arthur folded his arms. "Mrs. Cardigan wouldn't want to leave things up in the air. She's very thorough. She's arranged everything with Dr. Fugue."

Binky's mouth dropped open. "Dr. Fugue? No way!"

"Well, yes," said Arthur.

"I can't believe it!" said Binky. "You're going to be taught by Dr. Frederique Fugue? Boy, some kids get all the breaks."

"He's that good?" asked Arthur.

"Good? He's not just good. He's the *best*! If there were piano teachers on Mount Rushmore, he'd be the first head. I'd give anything for just one lesson with him. Even without the cookies. And I don't even play piano."

"Really?" Arthur looked pleased. "I had no idea. I guess it's an honor."

"I'll say." Binky rubbed his chin. "Of course, it will be a challenge. Your fingers might break from all the scales he makes you do."

"It can't be that bad," said Arthur. "You're just exaggerating."

Binky laughed. "Am I? Try telling that to my friend Mikey! He took lessons with Dr. Fugue for three months, and he still can't hold an ice-cream cone with only one hand."

Arthur put his own hands in his pockets.

"Oh," said Binky, "and one more thing. Watch out for the knitting needles."

"Knitting needles?" Arthur took a deep breath. "Dr. Fugue uses knitting needles during the lessons?"

Binky nodded.

"What for?" Arthur asked.

"You don't want to know. Just make sure you stay on the beat." Binky paused. "Good ol' Fugue the Ferocious. I admire your courage, Arthur."

Arthur frowned. "I don't want you admiring my courage. Well, I do, I suppose, but not in this case. I don't want to need courage for piano lessons."

"Well, it's too late now," said Binky. "Be brave, be fearless, and most of all, BEWARE!"

Chapter 3

"This is the place."

"Are you sure?"

Mr. Read checked his directions.

"It's the right number. And this is the only old Victorian house on the block. Do you want me to go in with you?"

Arthur shook his head. "No, I'll be okay."

He got out of the car and walked to the front door. Before he could even knock, though, the door swung open.

A tall, pale man with long limp hair stood before him. He extended a spidery hand in welcome.

"Arthur Read, I presume."

"That's me."

Arthur extended his own hand, but instead of shaking, Dr. Fugue pulled Arthur's hand up to his nose for a closer look.

"Hmmm . . . Moderate digital spreading and no calluses. I imagine you've been playing for . . . two-and-a-half years."

"Y-yes," said Arthur.

"Thought so," said Dr. Fugue. "Follow me."

As they went inside, Arthur heard his father honking a farewell.

Dr. Fugue cringed. *"Ech!* C-sharp. He should get that tuned."

They moved on to the living room. Arthur noticed holes in the rug and stuffing coming out of the wing chair.

A bird tweeted in a cage by the window. Dr. Fugue clapped his hands at her.

"Adagio, Tosca, *adagio!"*

The bird looked nervous and tweeted more slowly.

Although the rest of the room was a mess, the grand piano was a gleaming masterpiece.

"Wow!" said Arthur. "It's beautiful."

Dr. Fugue ran a finger over its surface, checking for dust. "Her name is Giselle. She's been around the world with me — from Vienna to Carnegie Hall."

Arthur's mouth dropped open. "You've actually played at Carnegie Hall?"

"Yes, yes, many times. But that's enough chitchat. Let's hear you play."

Arthur sat down at the piano while Dr. Fugue paced behind him.

"We'll start with some scales. D major!"

Arthur began to play.

"All right. Now C harmonic major . . . A minor . . . D major again."

The time flew by, but Arthur had no

chance to notice. He was too busy jumping from one demand to another.

"Tem-po! Tem-po! Tem-po!" snapped Dr. Fugue.

Finally, when Arthur felt like his fingers might begin falling off his hands altogether, Dr. Fugue said the magic words.

"And . . . stop!"

Arthur took a deep breath. Then another. And a third.

"That'll do for today. It appears that you might actually have some talent, Mr. Read. Therefore, I'd like you to work on this for next week's lesson."

He handed Arthur a book of music.

Arthur gasped. "But this is Bach's Two-Part Inventions. It has, like, a million notes."

"No, no, only eight thousand, nine hundred and fifty-five. And each of them is perfect. Let's begin with the Invention in F major."

Arthur stood up from the piano. "Um, I'm not so sure I can . . ."

He stopped because Dr. Fugue had reached into a basket and pulled out a pair of knitting needles.

"Genius is one percent inspiration and ninety-nine percent perspiration. So, naturally, you must practice. Now, what were you saying?"

Arthur's face had paled. "Um, nothing. Invention in F major. Right."

He snatched up his coat, mumbled a hasty good-bye, and ran out the front door.

Chapter 4

Arthur sat at his piano, staring at the music in front of him.

"Eight thousand, nine hundred and fifty-five notes," he muttered. "Mrs. Cardigan would never have given me something so hard. Just looking at this makes me tired."

He closed his eyes, but instead of seeing blackness, a line of half notes and quarter notes danced in front of him.

"Wheeeeee!"

Arthur opened his eyes. That was D.W.'s voice. It was coming from outside. Arthur got up and looked out the window.

"Just to make sure she's all right," he told himself.

D.W. seemed to be fine. She had collected a large pile of leaves and was jumping in them.

"Wheeeeee!" she shouted again.

Arthur frowned. It wasn't fair that he should be cooped up inside while D.W. had all the fun. Besides, when it came to jumping in leaves, her technique was not perfect. A little sister could use a big brother's greater experience to guide her.

And out he went.

The next day Arthur planned to practice again, but Francine rang the doorbell just as he was heading for the piano. She wanted to play football, and how could he let down a friend in need?

Two days later there was a book fair. Arthur couldn't miss that. Everyone knew how important reading was. Arthur made sure he explored the fair from one end to the other.

It didn't take many more excuses before five days had passed. On Saturday morning Arthur was making breakfast and outlining his day.

"First I'm going to help Buster carve his pumpkin. Then I'll —"

"Hold on a minute, Arthur," said his mother. "I think you're forgetting something."

"Oh, right, Mom. Buster asked me to bring that special carving tool."

"I didn't mean that. I mean the piano. You do remember the piano, don't you?"

"Of course," Arthur said slowly, the dancing notes appearing again in his head.

"Well, your lesson with Dr. Fugue is in two days, and I don't think you've practiced at all."

TUCKER
crunch

"Well, I've thought about practicing," said Arthur. "I've thought about it a lot. Doesn't that count?"

"Do you think it will count with Dr. Fugue?" asked his father.

An image of knitting needles suddenly replaced the dancing notes in Arthur's head. "No," he admitted, "I guess not."

"And this is your first real lesson together," his mother reminded him. "You want to make a good impression."

"I didn't have to worry about that with Mrs. Cardigan. It's not fair."

His mother smiled. "You may not remember, Arthur, but there was a time when playing for Mrs. Cardigan made you nervous, too."

"One hour," said Mr. Read. "Your fingers will thank you."

"What about —"

"Buster's pumpkin can wait. And you'll

have to do another hour tonight to really catch up."

"But . . . but . . ."

"No 'buts,' Arthur." Mr. Read stared at him. "Finish your cereal and get going."

Chapter 5

Arthur sat down at the piano, an oven timer at his side. He set it for one hour. "Sixty minutes and counting . . . ," he said.

He started to play, trying a few notes with only his right hand. His fingers moved awkwardly, stumbling over the keys.

"That's okay," he told himself. "Just take it one step at a time."

Suddenly, he heard a cow mooing.

"Huh?"

Then a pig oinked.

Both of these noises had come from the living room. Arthur tried to ignore them, but they were soon joined by whacking sounds.

"Take that!" he could hear D.W. saying. "And that!"

Arthur rushed into the living room to see what was going on. D.W. was sitting on the floor in front of a toy barn. Every time a farm animal appeared at a door or window, she tried to hit it with a plastic mallet.

"D.W., you're making too much noise. I'm trying to practice piano. Go play in your room."

"I can't. Mom is cleaning up in there."

Arthur folded his arms. "What will it take to keep you quiet?"

D.W. thought about it. "Got any candy?" she asked.

Arthur gave D.W. some of his Halloween candy and sat down again at the piano. He started again with his right hand, but just

when he was getting into it, he heard paper crackling.

"D.W.!"

"What?"

"You're still making too much noise."

D.W. walked in from the living room. "I can't help that. I have to unwrap the candy before I can eat it."

"Arrgghhh!" Arthur stomped off into the kitchen, where his father was just pulling out a tray of scones from the oven.

"Dad, I can't practice! D.W.'s making too much noise."

"Well, that's not good. I'll take her out. It's important for you to be able to concentrate."

"Thanks," said Arthur. "These smell great. A new recipe?"

"A slight variation," said his father. "Help yourself. And remember, no distractions."

Arthur piled a plate with scones, got a glass of milk, and returned to the living room. He heard the car pulling out of the driveway so he knew he was safe.

"Now I can play. But first I need my strength."

Arthur ate one scone, then another, then a third. He also drank the milk.

"Okay," he said, rubbing his hands together. "Invention in F Major, here we go."

He began playing again. Before long, though, he blinked a few times. Then he shook his head and stretched. That helped for a minute, but his eyelids grew heavier . . . and heavier . . . and heavier. He tried to open them, but it felt like someone had put a grand piano on each lid to hold it down.

Finally, he put his head down and fell asleep.

Riiinnnggggg!

Arthur awoke with a start as the oven timer went off. He looked at his watch and yawned.

"Oh. Practice is over. Well, that wasn't so bad."

Then he got up and went to see how Buster was doing with his pumpkin.

Chapter 6

When Arthur arrived again at Dr. Fugue's house, he noticed some pictures hanging on the wall.

"Hey! Is that you with Yo-Yo Ma?"

"Indeed," said Dr. Fugue. "Yo-Yo is a good friend of mine. Nobody plays the cello better."

"And who's the guy in the pink suit?"

"That's not a suit. It's a tuxedo studded with rhinestones. And the guy is Liberace. He used to be on television a lot, always in the most outrageous costumes. A lot of people didn't realize how good he was because they couldn't see past his clothes.

We had a dueling piano match when I was working my way through music school. But I digress. Let's hear that Bach!"

Arthur hesitated for a moment. "Are you sure you don't have more to tell me about Liberace? I'd be glad to listen."

"I'm sure you would," said Dr. Fugue. "But that's not why we're here." He gestured to the piano bench.

Arthur sat down. "You're sure this is a good time?" he asked.

"In point of fact," said Dr. Fugue, "it's the *only* time. Now, play!"

As expected, Arthur started with a few notes from Bach's Two-Part Invention in F major. Unfortunately, he did not play them in the exact order Bach had intended.

"Oops!" he said.

"Try again," said Dr. Fugue.

Arthur did. This time the notes came out even worse.

"Stop!" ordered Dr. Fugue. "Arthur, let

me pose a simple question to you. Did you practice this piece?"

"Yes, I did. Well, I mean, a little . . . kind of . . ." He sighed. "No, not really."

Dr. Fugue frowned. "Arthur, if you don't want to work at this, then I don't want to waste my time teaching you. I'm afraid you leave me no choice."

Arthur gasped. He was sure it was time for the knitting needles.

But instead Dr. Fugue simply led him to the front door.

"Good-bye, Arthur," he said. "You're fired."

The shock of that moment had faded somewhat once Arthur was working on his second chocolate milkshake at the Sugar Bowl. Buster was sitting across from him. He was on his second chocolate shake, too, but not because anything had happened to him. He just liked chocolate shakes.

ICE CREAM
CHIPS

"I can't believe it," said Buster. "You were fired by your piano teacher."

"Yeah." Arthur stirred his straw. "Just because I didn't play the piece perfectly."

"Wow. I'm sorry to hear that."

"My parents were, too. My father tried to argue with Dr. Fugue, but he didn't get anywhere."

"At least he tried," said Buster.

Arthur took another sip. "Of course, it's not all bad. It will take my parents a while to find me a new teacher. I won't have to practice for weeks. Maybe months."

"True." Buster looked impressed. "What will you do with all your free time?"

Arthur leaned back and clasped his hands behind his head. "I don't know. The possibilities are endless."

Chapter 7

It was raining, Arthur noted, as he looked out the window. It had been raining all morning, and judging by the way the sky looked, it was not giving up just yet.

Arthur drummed his fingers on the windowsill. The pitter-patter of the drops reminded him of the ticktock of the metronome. And thinking of that made Arthur think of the piano. But there was no point in that. So he turned away, plopped down on the couch, and turned on the TV.

"Amazing!" said the announcer, as a woman bowed beside a piano on a great stage. "A nearly flawless rendition of

Beethoven's 'Emperor' Concerto from Irina Verkova. We asked Irina before the performance how she got to Carnegie Hall. 'Practice,' she said."

Arthur switched the channel.

A disfigured man in an opera cape was playing a sad tune on an organ. His face was hidden by a mask.

"Oh, Phantom," sighed the damsel next to him. "You are so hideous, but you play so beautifully."

"There is no mystery in that, Christine. Until you came down to visit me in my underground lair, I had nothing but time on my hands. And with that time I practiced."

Arthur turned off the TV. He got up and wandered around, but no matter where he started, he always seemed to end up near the piano.

He played a single note and sighed. He thought about playing some more, but he felt silly somehow, playing for no one.

"Arthur!" his mother called out from the kitchen, "I'm going to the mall to buy socks."

He rushed into the kitchen to join her. "Can I come, too?" he asked. Anything was better than moping around like this. "Maybe we could look for coat hangers, too. We wouldn't want to run out."

The mall was its usual busy self, and Mrs. Read headed straight for The Sock Hop.

"I'll be next door," Arthur told her, heading for the music shop.

Inside, he was surrounded by instruments. And there, in the back, was a grand piano as shiny as a new pair of shoes.

Arthur sat down on the bench. "And now," he said softly, "Arthur Read will play Zuzukovski's Concerto Number Five."

He put down his fingers — and immediately hit a wrong chord.

SALE

A salesman dropped a pile of sheet music and rushed over.

"Excuse me, son, that's not a toy." He ushered Arthur out of his seat.

After that, Arthur felt pretty uncomfortable because he could feel the salesman watching him as he walked around.

As he stood by the door, another salesman was bringing a boy and his mother over to the same piano Arthur had been sitting at.

"Now," said the salesman, "I think this instrument may be suitable for Antoine."

"Give it an audition, Antoine," said his mother.

Antoine sat down, and with what seemed like no effort at all, he began playing Bach's Invention in F Major.

Arthur put his fingers in his ears and with his face turning red, he walked out.

Chapter 8

Mrs. Cardigan was sitting in her living room, surrounded by a sea of travel brochures.

"It's going to be quite the experience," she said. "The Albert Hall in London, La Scala in Milan. Paris. Vienna. Rome. Symphonies one night, operas the next. A few string quartets mixed in for good measure. I'm going to be in my glory, I can tell you that."

Arthur nodded. He wanted to say something nice, but his mouth was filled with chocolate-chip cookies.

"And then we're going to the factories.

PARIS
MILAN

Some people like to visit wineries, Arthur. I like to see where pianos are made."

Arthur swallowed some milk. "It sounds very exciting," he said.

"Yes, yes, Arthur. You're very polite." She paused. "But I know you didn't come to see me just to hear about my travel plans. And the cookies, though I know you like them, aren't enough of a draw, either. So, tell me, what's on your mind?"

Arthur cleared his throat. "Well, it's true I did want to ask you a question."

"Go on."

Arthur sat up straight in his chair. "Do you really think I have any talent? Playing the piano, I mean."

"Of course, you do, Arthur. That's why I sent you to Dr. Fugue."

"Oh."

Mrs. Cardigan put down her teacup. "How's that going, by the way?"

Arthur blushed. "Um, not so good. I guess Dr. Fugue kind of . . . uh . . ."

"Fired you?"

Arthur looked surprised. "How did you know?"

"He does that to a lot of students," said Mrs. Cardigan, waving her hand. "He's a brilliant teacher, but very demanding."

Hearing Mrs. Cardigan say that should have made Arthur feel better, but somehow it didn't. "The truth is," he said, "I was wondering how I could get him to unfire me."

"Hmmm . . . That's very difficult. It involves getting Dr. Fugue to change his mind. And his is not a mind that likes to change."

Arthur sighed. "So it's impossible, then."

"Oh, I didn't say that." She tapped her nose. "But there's only one way I can think of. You have to earn his respect."

"How can I do that?"

Mrs. Cardigan smiled. "By showing him what you're really capable of. I know what's inside you, Arthur, but he doesn't."

Arthur shook his head. "Right now it doesn't feel like there's anything inside me."

"Nonsense. You're here, aren't you? But remember, Arthur, you must play for yourself before you can play for anyone else."

"Especially Dr. Fugue."

Mrs. Cardigan laughed. "I suppose so."

"It still seems impossible," said Arthur. "Even his bird, Tosca, doesn't sing well enough for him."

Mrs. Cardigan took another sip of tea. "The beauty of it is, you don't have to play perfectly, Arthur. You just have to do your best."

Chapter 9

When Arthur got home, he was in a big hurry.

"How's Mrs. Cardigan doing?" asked his mother.

"Fine, fine. I'm kind of in a hurry, though. I've got a lot to do."

"I'm not surprised," said his mother. "There were five calls for you while you were gone."

Arthur hung up his jacket. "Any emergencies?" he asked.

"I don't think so."

"Nobody's in the hospital or anything?"

Mrs. Read shook her head. "Not that they mentioned."

"Good. I'll call them back later. Right now I'm busy."

"You are?"

He nodded. "I have a big meeting scheduled."

"A big meeting?"

Arthur nodded. "With eighty-eight keys," he explained.

Arthur meant it. He went straight to the piano and started practicing again. His fingers felt clumsy at first, but he just concentrated all the harder.

D.W. came in a little later. "Arthur, *Bionic Bunny* is on."

"I know. It's a repeat," Arthur answered.

"So? You always watch even though you know all the shows by heart."

"Not today, D.W. Now if you'll excuse me . . ."

D.W. ran back into the kitchen. "Mom!" she shouted. "I don't think Arthur's feeling well."

That night D.W. played with her farm animals again, but Arthur was so focused on his work that he didn't even hear her.

The next few days were much the same. Arthur spent all his free time at the piano. Buster came over to go bike riding, but Arthur told him to pedal his bike elsewhere. Francine showed up with her football, but Arthur said he would have to pass.

Even while he was sleeping, Arthur's fingers moved back and forth on his blanket.

Arthur kept on practicing. On Saturday he played through lunch and didn't even notice when his mother brought in a sandwich. He finally ate it, but when he thought about it afterward, he had no idea what kind of sandwich it had been.

As much as Arthur played, though, at

first he was very discouraged. It seemed like no sooner had he sort of learned one part than another part rose up like a wall before him.

I wonder if Bach had any trouble playing this himself, Arthur thought. He never did answer the question, but he chipped away at each wall bit by bit. After two weeks, there were not so many walls, and they came down faster. And in their place Arthur could follow the piece from beginning to end.

He thought about calling Dr. Fugue, and making another appointment, but every time he reached for the phone, he never quite managed to pick it up.

And then one day Arthur played the piece through from beginning to end, and for the first time he smiled.

"Well," he said, running his fingers down the keys, "I'm as ready as I'm ever going to be."

Chapter 10

Arthur walked up to Dr. Fugue's house carrying his music. The front door opened and a kid walked out. He looked sad until the door closed behind him. Then his expression changed.

"Whoopee! I've been fired!" He ran down the steps, skipping and leaping. Arthur shook his head. He walked slowly to the door and rang the bell.

The door swung open. "Ah," said Dr. Fugue. "Arthur Read. Dismissed for torturing the Invention in F Major if I remember correctly — and I always do. What brings you here?"

Arthur stared at the floor. "I know I should have called, but I was afraid you wouldn't see me."

"Quite right."

"That's why I decided just to come over. The truth is, I'd like another chance to play."

Dr. Fugue stroked his chin. "Hmmm . . . Most irregular. But seeing as how you had the nerve to make a return appearance, I will grant you another audition."

Back in Dr. Fugue's living room, everything looked as it had before. The furniture was the same, Tosca was the same, and the piano was the same.

Arthur sat down and began to play. He kept waiting for Dr. Fugue to stop him, to shout something, or slam his fist on the table.

But the doctor just watched him play.

When Arthur finished, he covered his face with his hands.

"Ugh! I must have made at least fifty mistakes."

"Seventy-eight, actually," said Dr. Fugue.

"Oh." Arthur stood up, dejected. "I'm sorry to have wasted your time, Dr. Fugue." He headed for the door.

Dr. Fugue cleared his throat. "Well, there is something that might improve your playing."

He reached into the basket that held the knitting needles. Arthur's eyes grew wide, not knowing what to expect.

"Here," said Dr. Fugue, handing him a pair of colorful gloves with holes for the fingers to poke through.

"I require all my students to keep their fingers warm," he explained.

Arthur took the gloves happily. His student! Dr. Fugue had called him *his student*. He might not be playing Carnegie Hall yet, but he sure was a whole lot closer.

"Now, let's play something together,"

BACH

said Dr. Fugue. He opened some music and beckoned Arthur to retake his seat.

As the notes from the music left the piano, the wind picked them up and carried them out the window. Away they went, tinkling on the breeze, until they finally crossed Mrs. Cardigan's porch, where she was sitting having a cup of tea.

"Ah," she said smiling, "my two star pupils playing together. Now that's music to my ears."